MR GREEN GROWS A GARDEN

by Ruth Owen

design and illustrations
by Emma Randall

with characters
by Tom Connell

RUBY TUESDAY BOOKS

In the middle of the big city, there was a tired, ugly place that made Mr Green feel very sad.

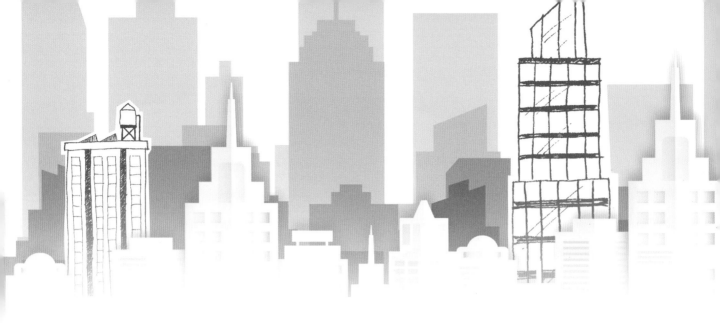

As he walked by one Friday afternoon, Mr Green stopped.

Like a tiny seed, an idea had sprouted in his head.

He picked up a plastic bottle . . .

. . . then another . . .

. . . and another. . . .

Mo was on his way home from school.

"What are you doing,
Mr Green?" he asked.

Mo and Mr Green were neighbours.

They lived three doors apart
on the third floor of the flats.

Every year on Mo's saddest day,
Mr Green brought flowers
for Mo and his mum.

That was the day Mo missed
his dad the most.

But Mr Green never forgot.

Mr Green stopped picking up rubbish.
"I am going to grow a garden here," he said.

"A garden for birds and bees and butterflies and toads and hedgehogs . . . and people!"

"Will you help me, young Mo?"

Mo gave Mr Green a big smile.

"Then we will begin work tomorrow," said Mr Green.

Mo could hardly wait for tomorrow. . . .

When tomorrow came, Mr Green and Mo got to work.
All weekend they picked up rubbish.

By Sunday teatime, they had also
collected lots of things
that Mr Green said ...

... would come in handy.

The next job was digging . . .

. . . and digging . . .

. . . and more digging.

All week, Mr Green dug the garden.
But something was wrong.

"The soil is not healthy," said Mr Green.

"What do you mean?" asked Mo.

"Soil is made up of tiny bits of rock," said Mr Green. "But to be healthy and feed plants, it needs lots of other ingredients."

Bits of animal bodies.

Dead leaves, flowers and rotting fruit.

The Ingredients For Soil

Worms, slugs, centipedes and insects.

Air and water

Animal poo

Soil contains microscopic living things called microbes. Microbes break down dead plants and other rotting matter and make them part of the soil.

Mo had a brilliant plan . . .

Mr Green's Garden Needs You!
Please bring:
Vegetable peelings
Eggshells
Dead leaves

. . . and soon the word spread.

The helpers at the city farm brought wheelbarrows of animal poo and straw.

Lots of tiny creatures came along for the ride!

Worms

Beetles

Springtails

Millipedes

Microbes

Some people brought leaves and grass clippings from their gardens.

And neighbours from the flats brought ...

banana skins

potato peelings

eggshells

mango skin

apple cores

chilli pepper stalks

carrot peelings

old hamster hay

toilet roll tubes

teabags

COMPOST

In a compost heap, old vegetables, fruit, weeds, twigs, leaves, cardboard and other waste rots. It becomes brown, crumbly compost that is very nutritious for plants.

... lots of good stuff for Mr Green's compost heap.

Mr Green and Mo dug . . .

. . . and dug . . .

. . . and dug the soil.

Soon the soil contained animal poo and straw.

Dead leaves

Compost from the compost heap

Worms and other tiny creatures

And more microscopic microbes than there are people on Earth!

Worms eat dead leaves and rotting stuff. Their poo becomes part of the soil and feeds plants.

Wriggling worms make tiny tunnels in the soil that let water trickle down to the roots of plants.

But someone was watching them dig.

There was a flash of bright red.

"That bird ate one of our worms!" cried Mo.

"Excellent," said Mr Green, smiling.
"Welcome to our garden, little robin."

The soil was ready!

Now Mr Green and Mo could grow some plants.

A seedling grows from a seed.

Sunflowers

Seeds come in many shapes and sizes.

Cabbage

Beetroot

Tomato

Pepper

Pea

Pumpkin

Sunflower

Onion

Carrot

Seedling

A carrot plant's root is the orange part we eat.

Bees, butterflies and other insects feed on sugary nectar from flowers.

Mo couldn't wait to get to the garden each weekend.

And every weekend, Mr Green taught him something new.

These tiny shoots will grow underground and make more potatoes.

Potato plants

Plants need sunlight to grow.

Pumpkin plant flower

A pumpkin starting to grow.

Dandelion

A plant's roots take in water and nutrients from the soil.

Weeds, such as dandelions, are tough, wild plants that grow quickly. Sometimes, gardeners pull them from the soil to stop them taking water and nutrients from other plants.

Each time he visited the garden,
Mo couldn't wait to get to work.

But this Saturday it was different.

It was Mo's saddest day.

"A garden isn't only for
gardening," said Mr Green.
"It's also a very good
place for thinking."

At first, Mo's head was empty.

But then it filled with thoughts and daydreams and memories.

Lots of happy memories.

A tomato plant grows from a seed.

Bees drink nectar from the tomato plant flowers.

A tiny fruit grows from each flower.

The fruits turn red.

Being in the garden made Mo want to smile.

"When will the garden be finished?" he asked one Saturday morning.

Mo didn't want the smiley feeling to end.

Mr Green laughed!

"A garden is never finished, young Mo," he said, smiling.

"There is always something to do and always something to look forward to."

Each tomato contains more seeds.

Strawberry plants

Beans

Bean pod

Beans and peas are seeds that grow inside pods.

A flower needs pollen from another flower to help it make seeds. Bees carry dusty pollen from flower to flower on their bodies.

Peas

Bean plants

Cucumber plant

Pea plants

This little seedling grows into a Brussels sprout plant.

Brussels sprouts

Toads hunt for slugs and worms to eat in gardens.

Mr Green's garden grew and grew.

One day, somebody left a gift for the garden.

"It's a young oak tree," said Mr Green.

The little plant didn't look much like a tree to Mo.

Mr Green handed Mo his spade.
"You should plant the tree, young Mo," he said.
"And then you will grow tall together!"

What does a tree do?

A tree releases oxygen from its leaves that people and animals need to breathe.

A tree's leaves remove carbon dioxide from the air.

An oak tree can be a home for birds, squirrels and hundreds of insects and spiders.

An oak tree may live for one thousand years.

In autumn, an oak tree's leaves fall to the ground and become food for worms, millipedes and other tiny animals.

An oak tree produces seeds called acorns that are food for squirrels, badgers, deer and birds.

Summer... Autumn... Winter... Spring...

...the seasons passed.

Mr Green's garden became a place for
smiles and chatter.

And laughter and new friends.

There was always something to do . . .

THE SHED

. . . and always something to look forward to.

Seed Swap FREE coffee & cake This Saturday!

The Garden Choir Sing-a-long

Sunday night 7pm

May 1st BIG Spring Get-together Bring a picnic

Winter... Spring... Summer... Autumn...

...Mr Green's garden grew and grew.

THE SHED

FREE APPLES & PUMPKINS

"It's cold today," said Mo, one autumn afternoon.

"Let's go home and have hot chocolate."

MO'S OAK TREE

"But I have so many things to finish," said Mr Green.

Mo smiled at his best friend. "Remember, Mr Green," he said. "A garden is never finished!"

In the middle of the big city, there would always be a beautiful green place.

And it made everyone feel very happy.

Remember! In a garden, there is always
something to look forward to. . . .